ERIC CARLE

The Foolish Tortoise

W9-CBJ-216

Written by Richard Buckley

READY-TO-READ

SIMON SPOTLIGHT

New York   London   Toronto   Sydney   New Delhi

This book was previously published with slightly different text.

SIMON SPOTLIGHT

An imprint of Simon & Schuster Children's Publishing Division

1230 Avenue of the Americas, New York, New York 10020

Text copyright © 1985 by Richard Buckley

Illustrations copyright © 1985 by Eric Carle

Originally published by Picture Book Studio in 1985

First Simon Spotlight Ready-to-Read edition May 2015

Eric Carle's name and signature logo type are registered trademarks of Eric Carle.

For information about special discounts for bulk purchases, please contact Simon & Schuster Special Sales
at 1-866-506-1949 or business@simonandschuster.com.

The Simon & Schuster Speakers Bureau can bring authors to your live event. For more information or to book
an event contact the Simon & Schuster Speakers Bureau at 1-866-248-3049 or visit our website at
www.simonspeakers.com.

Manufactured in the United States of America 0315 LAK

10 9 8 7 6 5 4 3 2 1

Library of Congress Cataloging-in-Publication Data

Buckley, Richard, 1938-

The foolish tortoise / by Richard Buckley ; illustrated by Eric Carle. — First edition.

pages cm. — (Ready-to-read. Level 2)

"First Simon Spotlight Ready-to-Read edition"—Copyright page.

Originally published with slightly different text by Picture Book Studio in 1985.

Summary: A tortoise realizes the need for a shell after several scary encounters.

[1. Stories in rhyme. 2. Turtles—Fiction.] I. Title.

PZ8.3.B8474Fo 2015

[E]—dc23

2014048738

ISBN 978-1-4814-3578-9 (hc)

ISBN 978-1-4814-3577-2 (pbk)

This book was previously published with slightly different text.

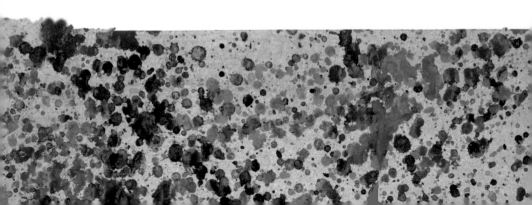

A tortoise was tired of being slow.
He wanted to get up and go.

He took off his large, heavy shell.
He left it lying where it fell.

"Hooray!" he cried.
"Now I have been freed.
I will see the world at double speed!"

He was faster, but not express,
and his protection was far less.

So when he heard a hornet's drone,
The tortoise crept beneath a stone.

A hungry bird came swooping past.
He looked so fierce and flew so fast.
The tortoise hid behind some trees
and felt quite weak behind the knees.

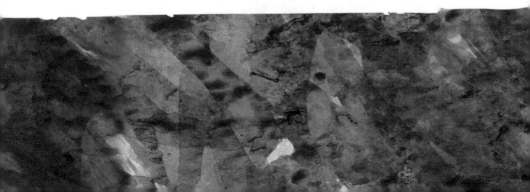

"I do not feel safe.
There is too much risk.
If only I could be more brisk!"

He headed for the riverbed.
A fish swam up and the tortoise fled.

Along his way our hero went,
and almost had an accident.

A snake with open jaws slid near.
The tortoise backed away in fear.

A hare, a hound, and a horse raced by
so rapidly they seemed to fly.

The tortoise gasped, eyes open wide.
I will never be that quick," he sighed.

He wandered on. The sun rose high.
"I wish I had more shade!" he cried.

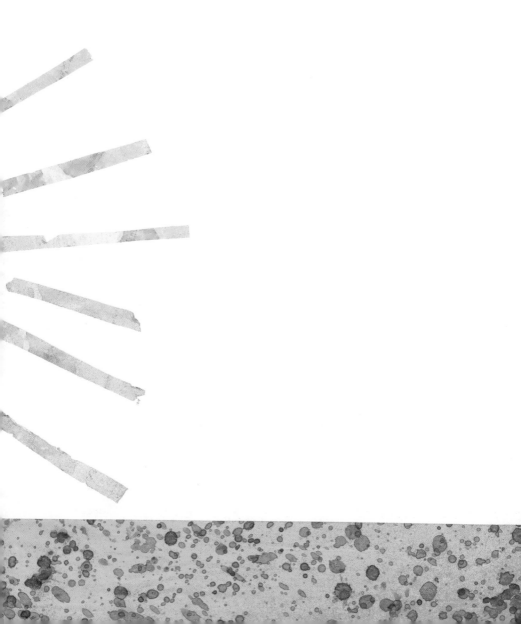

A sudden thunderstorm rolled in
and soaked the tortoise to the skin.

The wind rose up, and soon the breeze
was bending branches in the trees.

The tortoise shook. "Now I am cold.
I wish I had not been so bold."

"I think I have lost the urge to roam,
I think it is time that I went home.
Without my shell I do not feel right."

So when his shell came into sight,

He climbed back in and said,
"Good night!"